a minedition book
published by Penguin Young Readers Group

Text copyright © 2005 by Brigitte Weninger
Illustrations copyright © 2005 by Stephanie Roehe
First American edition, 2006
First published in German under the original title:
MIKO und der halbe Hund
translated by Charise Myngheer
Coproduction with Michael Neugebauer Publishing Ltd. Hong Kong.
All rights reserved. This book, or parts thereof,
may not be reproduced in any form
without permission in writing from the publisher,
Penguin Young Readers Group,
345 Hudson Street, New York, NY 10014.
The scanning, uploading and distribution of this book via the Internet or via any other means
without the permission of the publisher is illegal and punishable by law.
Please purchase only authorized electronic editions, and do not participate in or encourage
electronic piracy of copyrighted materials. Your support of the author's rights is appreciated.
Published simultaneously in Canada.

ISBN 0-698-40016-X

Manufactured in Hong Kong by Wide World Ltd.
Typesetting in Kidprint MT
Color separation by Fotoreproduzioni Grafiche, Verona, Italy.
Library of Congress Cataloging-in-Publication Data available upon request.

10 9 8 7 6 5 4 3 2 1
First Impression

Brigitte Weninger

MiKO
Wants
a Dog

Illustrated by

Stephanie Roehe

min dition

"Will you play with me?"
Miko asked his little friend Mimiki.
Mimiki nodded.
"Great, then you can pretend
to be my dog!"
said Miko.

Miko gave Mimiki-the-dog
a dog bowl and a bed.

Mimiki-the-dog played ball with Miko.

Mimiki-the-dog barked and wagged his tail.

But when Miko wanted to put a leash on him, Mimiki-the-dog got mad.
"No!" said Mimiki. "I don't want to play anymore!
I'm not really a dog!"

"Mom, can I pleeeeeease have a real dog?" begged Miko.

"Miko, you know we can't have a dog," said Mom.

"No one is home all day and the poor dog would be all alone."

Miko sat on the back step and pouted.

"When I get big, I'm going to get a dog," said Miko.

"No. Two dogs. One for me, and a tiny little dog for you!"

Mimiki thought that was a great idea.

Suddenly, a surprising sound came from the yard next door.
Mimiki heard it too.
Miko and Mimiki peeked through the hedge.
Mrs. Miller was standing in her yard beside a...

... a dog! A real, live, loud-barking, tail-wagging dog!
Mrs. Miller was trying to dry the dog's paws,
but the little dog just wanted to play.

"Hey, Mrs. Miller," called Miko. "When did you get a dog?"

"Today," answered Mrs. Miller. "We're just getting to know each other."

"Should I help you?" asked Miko.

When Mrs. Miller nodded yes, Miko and Mimiki quickly squeezed through the hedge.

"What's his name?" asked Miko.

"His name is Lil Max," said Mrs. Miller.

Miko held the fidgety dog by the collar and said in a firm voice, "Sit, Lil Max!"

Lil Max immediately sat down and let Miko dry off his paws.

"You seem to know a lot about dogs," said Mrs. Miller.

"Yeah," agreed Miko. "That's because I love dogs!"

Miko rubbed Lil Max behind the ears.
"Lil Max's fur is wet too," said Miko. "Should I
dry him off and brush him?"
"That would be a big help," said Mrs. Miller.
"Come on inside."

Lil Max had a dog bowl and a bed.
Lil Max played ball with Miko.
Lil Max barked and wagged his tail.
And when Miko put the leash on
Lil Max, he didn't get mad.

Lil Max wanted to go for a walk
and ran to the door.

"See Mimiki, this is how a real dog acts!" said Miko.

That was just fine with Mimiki. He liked riding on Lil Max's back more than being on a leash. The three friends went for a walk in the yard.

"Good dog," said Miko.

"Miko, you are a good helper!" said Mrs. Miller.

When Miko got home, he was so happy.
He hugged his mom and said, "Guess what!
I have a dog! A REAL DOG!
He lives with Mrs. Miller, and she said
that because I'm such a good helper,
Lil Max belongs to me too!"
"How wonderful," said Mom. "You are a
good helper, Miko!"

For more information about MIKO & Mimiki and our other books, please visit our website: www.mineedition.com